Chapter 4

A small monkey watched them from the branches. It heard them planning and wanted to help.

"Excuse me?" it called from above.

Himmat and Jai wondered where the voice had come from.

"Up here!" the monkey called again.

"You're a monkey!" said Jai.

"Very observant of you," the monkey replied. "I know where the circus is."

"Really?"

Himmat and Jai looked at each other in excitement.

"Yes," said the monkey. "I can show you. But before I do, you must make me a promise."

Himmat's father growled. "We don't make promises!" he bellowed. "Just tell us!"

The monkey shrugged. "Fine," it said. "Find it yourselves – "

"Father!" groaned Himmat. "Just listen!"

The monkey smiled. "The circus took many animals from the jungle. It even stole some of my friends. You must promise to let all the animals go."

Himmat looked at her father. A moment passed.

"Agreed," her father replied.

"And you *have* to let them escape," the monkey added. "You can't *eat* any of them."

Himmat's brother groaned. "Where's the fun in that?" asked Dev.

"*Promise!*" said the monkey.

One by one, the tigers solemnly agreed.

"I promise, too," said Jai.

The animals burst into laughter. Himmat was so amused, she rolled around on the floor.

"Silly human – I'm not scared of you, Jai!" said the monkey. "So, do we have a deal?"

"Yes," said Himmat.

The monkey nodded. "I'll stay in the low branches," it said. "You can follow me."

"Why don't you come down here?" asked Himmat.

"Because I am a monkey and you are tigers," it replied. "I'm not that silly!"

Dev groaned again.

"Fine, let's go," said Himmat.

Jai, Himmat and her family followed the brown-furred primate deeper into the jungle. According to the monkey, the circus was near another village.

"We have to get to the river," the monkey added.

"There's a river?" asked Jai.

"You humans don't know anything, do you?" the monkey replied. "The circus travels along the river. They have barges and boats. It's easier than hacking through the jungle."

They walked for a whole hour until Jai heard water. His feet ached and he was hungry.

"Can we rest?" he asked.

"Only for a moment," said the monkey. "We need to keep moving."

Following the riverbank was easier. There were fewer bushes and trees, and a narrow path. But it still took another hour before the village appeared.

"Quick, hide!" said Himmat. "Don't let them spot us!"

They took cover in the bushes and rested again. Jai could see three barges and a boat, about a kilometre along the river. The barges were big and loaded with wooden crates and covered metal cages. The boat was smaller. On the bank, three big, brightly-coloured tents had been set up. One was blue, one red and one yellow.

"The circus!" whispered Jai.

He was excited now. He had imagined going on adventures for many years. Now, here he was, having an actual adventure! With a monkey and some tigers!

Just wait until his mum found out …

"Oh," he said.

"What's the matter?" asked Himmat.

"I didn't tell my mother," he replied. "She will be worried when she realises I'm missing."

"We didn't think of that," said Himmat.

The monkey tried to reassure Jai with a smile. "Don't fear," it said. "Once we free the animals, I'll take you home."

"So, what do we do now?" asked Himmat.

Her father stood. "You can all wait here," he said. "I'll take a look."

"But what if they see you?" asked Jai.

The tiger shook his giant head. "They won't," he replied. "I'm very good at hiding. Don't move from this spot. I'll be back soon."

As they waited, the monkey went to find some food. It returned with bananas and berries.

"I'm not eating those!" said Dev. "I'm a tiger, not a mouse!"

"Fine," said the monkey. "You can starve."

Jai was grateful for his banana and wolfed it down in two bites.

"Delicious!" he said. "Can I have another one?"

Himmat ate hers quickly, too. Dev watched them, his stomach rumbling with hunger.

"Is it tasty?" he eventually asked his sister.

"*Very* tasty," said Himmat. "The berries are great, too!"

"Oh well, I suppose it won't do any harm," said Dev. "May I have a banana?"

The monkey threw one at him.

"I knew you'd change your mind," it said. "I'll go and find some more."

Himmat turned to Jai. "Thanks for coming with us," she said. "You didn't have to."

"I know," Jai replied. "But I wanted to help. And I wanted an adventure, too. I just hope my mother will understand."

"I'm sure she will," said Himmat. "She'll probably think you're a hero!"

"Maybe," said Jai, but he wasn't so sure.

Himmat's father returned a while later.

"Did you find Mother?" asked Himmat.

"I didn't see her," he replied. "But I spoke to an elephant, who confirmed that she's here. They have her in the yellow tent. She's part of the show."

"The show?" asked Jai.

"The Tiger and the Strongman," Himmat's father explained. "They make her wrestle with a human, to amuse the crowd. The animals are treated badly and the circus owner is very mean."

"*GRRRRRRR!*" said Himmat. "We'll see who's mean!"

They stared at her in shock.

"What's the matter?" she asked.

"That is the best growl you've ever made!" said her father.

"Really?"

He nuzzled her forehead with his snout. "That's my girl!" he replied.

"So, what now?" the monkey asked.

"They have a show this evening," said Himmat's father. "We wait."

"*And –* ?" the monkey added.

"We go in and save them," said Himmat. "What else?"

"Yes," said the monkey, wondering if all tigers were so silly, "but *how* do we do that?"

"I don't know," said Himmat.

Jai grinned. "I do!" he said. "I will go and set the animals free. I'm human, so they won't suspect me."

"What do I do?" asked Himmat.

"You can protect me," said Jai. "Be a good tiger!"

"*GRRRRRRRRR!*" roared Himmat.

BONUS

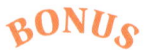

Indian circuses

Empire Circus

The Empire Circus dates from 1880 and is one of India's oldest circuses. It was known for its animal performances, clown shows and trapeze acts.

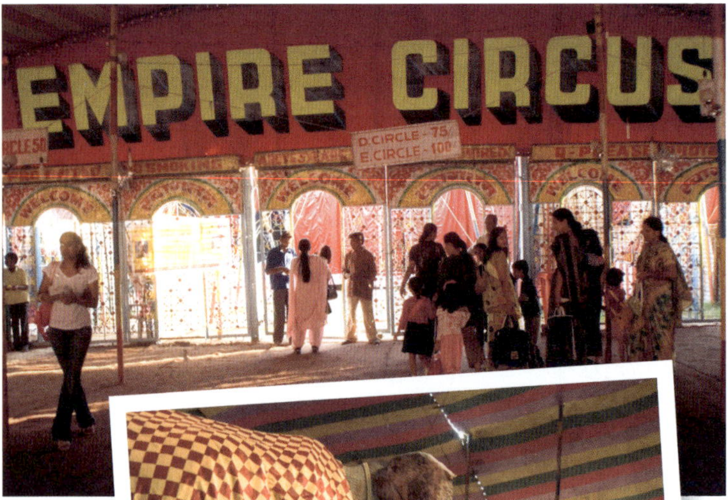

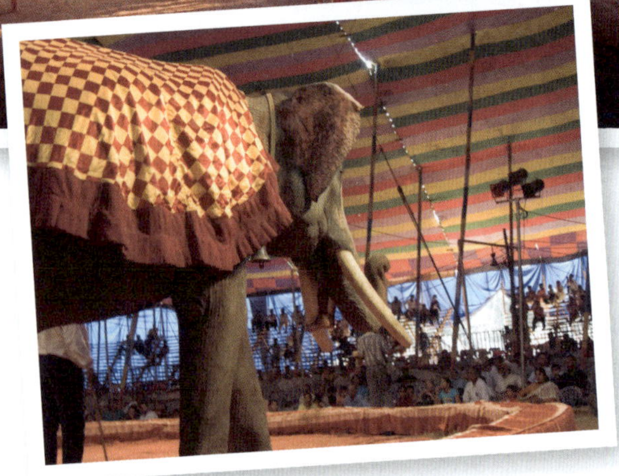

The Great Bombay Circus

The Great Bombay Circus started in 1920 and featured acrobats, jugglers, and animal feats.

Rambo Circus

Since 1991, the Rambo Circus has demonstrated acrobatics and risk-taking exploits, such as fire-eating.

Chapter 5

Later that evening, Jai and Himmat crept into place. Jai was sweating and scared. What if they were discovered? Or one of them got hurt?

"Are you ready?" whispered Himmat.

"I think so," replied Jai.

The circus ground was bustling with people, and no one saw them hiding in the shadows behind the yellow tent.

"Let me take a look," said Jai. "You wait here."

Nervously, he stood up and joined the crowds. He was looking for the owner, or at least someone with keys. The yellow tent hadn't opened yet, so he made his way towards the red one.

As he approached, he heard a whistle. Looking up, he saw the monkey hanging from some rope above him. It jumped onto his shoulder.

"Most of the animals are already performing," it said. "So, this will be easier than we think. You just need to set the big elephants free. Once they charge, nothing can stop us!"

"Where are they?"

"Behind the blue tent," said the monkey, disappearing again.

Jai looked into the red tent and saw a troupe of monkeys, dressed in silly clown outfits, performing for the audience. A stern-looking man ordered the monkeys around. A set of keys hung from his waistband. The audience seemed to love the show.

"Get on with it, you wretched animals!" the man cried.

Jai wanted to stop him, but he had to stick to the plan. Instead, he left and made his way to the blue tent.

Inside, two small elephants were parading around a sawdust ring, carrying monkeys and apes on their backs. In the middle, a leopard roared at them. Again, the audience cheered and clapped, and Jai grew confused. Why were they entertained by such cruelty? It made no sense.

"No wonder animals fear us," he whispered.

"*Hmmmm?*" said a woman nearby.

"Nothing," replied Jai.

"I can't wait to see the Tiger and the Strongman," said the woman. "I've heard it's the best show in the country!"

"Oh," said Jai. "I'm sure tonight's show will be the best one ever."

He grinned to himself and walked on, eager to find the elephants. As he walked around the blue tent, he heard them before he saw them. They were trumpeting and pounding their feet, as a circus worker cracked her whip.

"What's going on?" a woman demanded. "Have you elephants lost your minds?"

But nothing she did would calm them.

"I'm going to have a quick break," she told the animals. "You'd better be ready when I return or you will suffer the consequences!"

Irritated, she turned and fled, dropping a set of keys as she did so.

Jai waited until the woman was gone to pick up the keys. The elephants saw him and continued to complain.

"SSSSHHH!" urged Jai. "I've come to free you!"

Both elephants stopped and stared at him.

"But you're a human," said one.

"Yes," said Jai. "And I'm here with the tigers."

The elephants were tied with chains, around their necks and back legs. Jai worked quickly, unlocking and unravelling chain after chain, hoping that the woman would not return.

"WHAT ARE YOU DOING, BOY!"

He was too late. The woman rushed towards him.

"*Nooooo!*" Jai cried.

Suddenly, the bigger elephant broke free of the last chain and knelt.

"On my back, human!" it said. "Let's show them what elephants can do!"

The woman immediately halted and her eyes grew wide in fear.

The second elephant also broke free of its remaining chains. "Where's your whip now?" it demanded.

The woman screamed, turned and ran, catching an oil lamp as she went. The lamp smashed and the straw around it caught fire. The blaze erupted quickly and soon spread towards the blue tent. The audience shouted and screamed and scampered for safety.

"Come on!" Jai yelled at the elephants. "We have to hurry!"

As the blue tent caught fire, Dev and the monkey were busy, too. They had crept into the red tent. Dev waited for his moment and pounced, pinning the circus master to the floor.

"GRRRRRRRRRRRR!!!!!!!"

The man squealed in fright and began to sob. As the audience fled, the monkey took the circus master's keys.

"I'll set the rest of the animals free," he said.

By the time Jai rode past on his elephant, the red tent was collapsing. Humans were running in every direction. The monkey jumped up on the elephant, too.

"Just the yellow tent left!" the elephant said.

"We must hurry," said Jai. "The flames will destroy everything."

"You weren't supposed to start a fire!" said the monkey.

"It wasn't us!" Jai replied.

The elephant moved on, careful not to crush any humans. Instead, it broke the last poles holding up the red tent.

"One more to go!" it yelled.

The fire raged quickly behind them as the animals shrieked and the humans screamed. The flames were moving fast, and Jai prayed that no one would be hurt. They only wanted to teach the humans a lesson.

Himmat was waiting by the yellow tent. "I haven't seen my mother!" she growled. "Where is she?"

Jai looked towards the flames. "I don't know, but the flames are getting closer!" he said.

The elephant trumpeted to sound the alarm. "It's too late!" it said. "We have to go before we're trapped by the blaze!"

Himmat looked bewildered and distraught, but realised she had no choice. "MOTHER!" she bellowed one last time.

Moments later, a roar rang out in response. It was Himmat's father. A second roar followed.

"MOTHER?" cried Himmat. "That's my mother!"

Behind them, the yellow tent caught fire, too. The rope tying it down crackled and split. The roof fell in with a *whoosh*.

"RUN!" yelled the elephant.

Suddenly, Himmat's father burst snarling from the burning tent. Then another tiger appeared. This one was almost as big and carried a human on its back. Jai nearly fell off the elephant in shock.

"FATHER????"

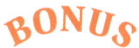

BONUS

African elephants

African elephants have rounded heads and very large ears.

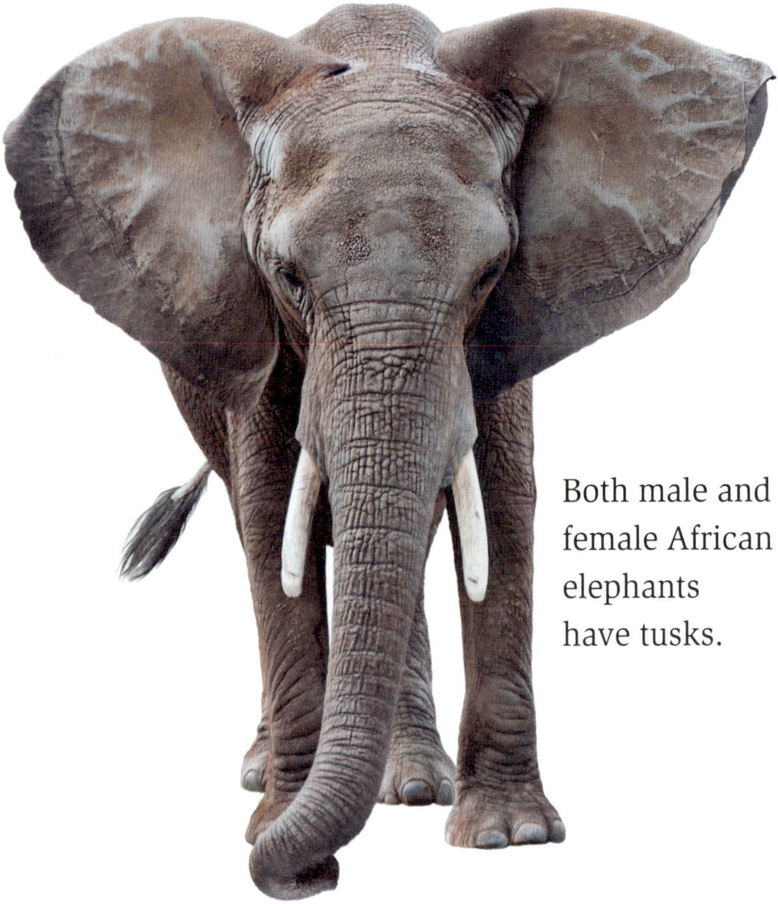

Both male and female African elephants have tusks.

Asian elephants

Asian elephants have double-domed head shapes and smaller ears.

Only male Asian elephants have tusks.

Chapter 6

They made for the river, as the circus tents burned. Once there, Jai jumped from his elephant and rushed to hug his father.

"I can't believe it!" he shouted, as his father lifted him into the air.

"What is going on?" his father asked.

"We came to rescue Himmat's mother and then the fire started and then you appeared and – " Jai fought to find his breath.

"Calm down," his father advised. "You're with these animals?"

Jai nodded quickly. "But why are *you* here?" he asked.

Jai's father shrugged. "I was looking for wood in the jungle," he explained. "That's when I saw Rani being captured and I decided to join the circus temporarily to see if I could free her."

"Rani?" asked Jai.

Himmat nudged him. "He means my mother," she said.

The fire was still raging towards them. Jai's cheeks were red from the heat.

"The circus owners created a show where we fought each other," Jai's father told him. "But we became friends, so we didn't hurt each other. The people loved the show and we ended up working for the circus master."

The monkey shrieked at them. "Perhaps we can discuss this later," it said. "Time to go!"

The elephants thanked the tigers and the humans and walked into the jungle. The monkeys howled and laughed and disappeared into the branches. The other animals also melted away into the bushes. The fire, unable to reach the trees because of the river, began to die down. In the distance, Jai saw the circus master and his crew hurtling towards them. They looked incandescent with rage.

Dev growled and got ready to attack, but his mother stopped him. "Let's just go."

Jai's father told them to board the smaller boat. "It has a motor," he said. "And we'll get back much quicker along the river."

"What if the men follow us?" asked Himmat.

"If we take the small boat, they can't," said Jai's dad. "They use it to pull the barges along."

They climbed aboard and Jai's father started the engine. The motor roared and then they were off. As they sped away, the circus master loitered helplessly on the shore, cursing them. Behind him, two leopards crouched, ready to pounce …

It was morning by the time Jai and his father trudged back into their village. Their neighbours cheered in delight and amazement.

"You're alive!" they shouted.

"Thank heavens!" they exclaimed.

As they forced their way through the crowds, Jai wondered where his mother was.

"JAI!" he heard her shout.

She ran to him and enveloped him in her arms. When she saw her husband, her mouth fell open and she began to cry. "How can this be?" she asked. "I thought you'd been – "

"I'm fine," Jai's father replied. "Jai rescued me."

"Rescued? From what?" his mother asked.

She took Jai's face in her hands. "Tell me everything," she demanded.

"Later," said Jai. "I'm hungry and I need a bath."

His mother smiled. "You *and* your father," she said. "You smell of animals and straw and smoke. Where have you been?"

"On an adventure," Jai revealed. "Like the ones I dreamed about. With monkeys and elephants and tigers. Kind tigers!"

"Tigers, eh?" she replied, looking at his father.

"He's not lying," his father replied. "There were *definitely* tigers."

Jai's mum laughed. "What a pair you are," she said.

Jai sat in the jungle a week later, feeling contented. He hadn't felt this happy in ages. Having his father back felt wonderful. It was a dream come true. And being the hero felt amazing, too. Everyone wanted to ask him about it. Now, seeking peace and quiet, he sat alone and thought of Himmat. He imagined her chasing around after her mother, as happy as he was. It was an intoxicating feeling.

"*Mmmm*, lunch is here," he heard her say behind him.

He jumped from the rock and hugged her. "My friend!" he said. "I was just thinking about you!"

"And I was thinking about you," she replied. "I came here yesterday, hoping you might have come."

"I wanted to," said Jai, "but I was too busy. Since the rescue, everyone wants to hear my story. And my father's relatives have visited every day."

"Do you have many relatives?" asked Himmat.

"*Hundreds*," said Jai, pulling a face. "It's getting very boring. Father loves it, though. It must be wonderful to be free."

"My mother is the same," Himmat told him. "She's done nothing but sleep and snore and smile, since we returned."

They giggled and decided to take a walk through the jungle.

"I wanted to say goodbye," Himmat eventually said.

"Goodbye?"

She nodded and nuzzled Jai's arm. "We are going further into the jungle," she replied. "Maybe even to the other side."

"But why?" asked Jai. "I don't want you to leave!"

"I don't want to leave either," said Himmat. "We have no choice. The humans are too close."

"But we're not all bad people," Jai told her.

"That is true," she said. "But we can't risk being caught again. Or worse – "

Jai understood Himmat's concerns. He just didn't like it.

"I'll miss you," he said.

"I'll miss you, too," she replied. "Maybe you could come and find me when you become an explorer?"

"But where will you be?" asked Jai.

The monkey chose that moment to drop from a nearby tree with bananas. "I'll know," it said.

"Monkey!" they exclaimed.

"Friends! I wanted to say thank you – with bananas."

They chuckled, then sat and ate.

"Can you really find Himmat?" asked Jai.

"I can find anything," the monkey replied. "I see everything from up there."

"Then that's settled," said Himmat.

Jai nodded. "You could have eaten me," he said.

"But I didn't," Himmat replied.

"If you had, our parents would still be missing."

"Exactly," said Himmat.

"Here's to being kind, then!" Jai replied.

"Oh, stop talking rubbish and eat your bananas!" said the monkey.

Jai grinned and cuddled his friends.

"The boy and the tiger," he said. "And the monkey, too!"

DAILY
BONUS

Missing man returns!

A jungle village is in a full-swing celebration as a man who had gone missing in the jungle six weeks previously has returned. Kamal Devi, 34, was seen walking back into the village in the early hours of yesterday morning with his son Jai Devi, 10.

He had allegedly become caught up with the travelling circus that has been making its way north across the country. His wife, son and all the villagers are overjoyed that he is back fit and well and Kamal has said he feels "very lucky" to be back home.

NEWS

About the author

Did you always want to be a writer?

Yes, ever since I was seven years old. I wrote every day as a child and wanted to be just like the authors I read. My hero was Sue Townsend – she was amazing, both as a writer and as a human. I wanted to follow in her footsteps.

Bali Rai

What's your favourite thing about writing?

Starting a new story – it's the best bit! I love coming up with new ideas and then working on them. Not every idea becomes a story, but the fun is in trying to write them. I love developing characters, too. Thinking about who they are and why they take part in the story.

How did you come up with the idea for this story?

I watched a documentary about Indian tigers years ago and wanted to write something about tigers ever since. This was my chance to do that! Tiger populations are falling quickly and, as humans, we must take caring for nature more seriously. We aren't the most important species on our planet. It is an ecosystem of many species that only works properly if we are all allowed to exist.

How do you come up with ideas for stories?
I am inspired by the world and the people around me. That's where most of my ideas come from. I'm also inspired by every story I read and enjoy. The world is full of stories — some set nearby, and others set far away. I write about ordinary people facing extraordinary challenges.

What's important to you about this story?
The story is about friendship, empathy and being kind. Kindness leads to wonderful things and was the main theme for me. It's also about humans driving animal species out of their homes, and how awful that is. Humans must learn to co-exist with animals.

Have you ever seen any of these animals?
I've seen monkeys and elephants in the wild, and also lizards, but never tigers, sadly. I've even been to Brazil, for work, but didn't manage to visit the Amazon rainforest. I'd love to explore a jungle environment properly. Maybe I'd discover a lost temple or an unknown animal species! I can dream!

What do you hope readers will get out of the book?
I hope readers will think about the importance of kindness in our everyday lives. And perhaps empathise with the plight of animals as humans expand into their habitats. We must share our world with nature, not replace it.

About the illustrator

Did you always want to be an illustrator?

I have always loved drawing. I also loved reading picture books and graphic novels but never imagined I'd become a professional illustrator until I had the opportunity to illustrate my first picture book. Once I did, there was no turning back – a new world had opened up and my journey continues.

Debasmita Dasgupta

How did you get into illustrating?

A publisher in New Delhi, India, asked me to illustrate a picture book for them. At that time I was working with the United Nations in international relations with practically no experience in children's book illustration. That was in 2010 when there were not many places to learn picture book illustration. However, while illustrating that book, I knew that illustrating was what I wanted to do. It took me a while to hone my skills and in 2017, I became a full-time illustrator.

Do you have a favourite medium?

I love the combination of digital outlines and colours with hand-painted textures and motifs. Sometimes, I use original fabrics and digitally integrate them in my artwork.

How do you go about illustrating a book like this?

First, I read the story and imagine the characters.
To me, characters are the main building blocks of an illustrated story. And by characters I don't just mean humans. They could be humans, animals, aliens – anything that carries the story on its shoulders. The more I understand the details of these characters, the better I'm able to create my illustrations.

What was your favourite part of this book to illustrate?

Drawing Himmat. I love her! She's young, vulnerable, but she is also brave and full of life.

Does anything you've drawn relate to your own life or experiences?

I was born in the city of Kolkata in the east of India, which is very close to the Sundarbans, where this story is set. I have grown up hearing folk tales, as well as true stories about the Royal Bengal Tiger.

Do you relate to any of the characters in the book?

The people of the Sundarbans and that landscape hold a very special place in my heart. I have visited there, lived there and worked there. Reading this story felt like reliving many of those unforgettable moments of my life.

What advice would you give someone who wants to be a book illustrator?

Read the text lots of times. Understand what the story is trying to communicate and who the main audience is. That way, your illustrations will enhance the story.

Book chat

What was your favourite part of this book?

Do any of the characters change from the beginning of the story to the end? How?

Would you like to go to the jungle? Why or why not?

What do you think the tigers learnt about people and the people learnt about tigers?

What do you think happens next in the story?

If you had to think of a new title for this book, what would you choose?

Do you have a favourite character in the book? If so, who and why?

If you could speak to the author, what would you ask?

Book challenge:

Draw a missing poster for either Jai's father or Himmat's mother.

Published by Collins
An imprint of HarperCollins*Publishers*

The News Building
1 London Bridge Street
London
SE1 9GF
UK

Macken House
39/40 Mayor Street Upper
Dublin 1
D01 C9W8
Ireland

© HarperCollins*Publishers* Limited 2025

10 9 8 7 6 5 4 3 2 1

ISBN 978-0-00-876790-7

All rights reserved. No part of this publication may be reproduced, stored in a retrieval system, or transmitted in any form by any means, electronic, mechanical, photocopying, recording or otherwise, without the prior written permission of the Publisher or a licence permitting restricted copying in the United Kingdom issued by the Copyright Licensing Agency Ltd, 5th Floor, Shackleton House, 4 Battle Bridge Lane, London SE1 2HX.

Without limiting the exclusive rights of any author, contributor or the publisher of this publication, any unauthorised use of this publication to train generative artificial intelligence (AI) technologies is expressly prohibited. HarperCollins also exercise their rights under Article 4(3) of the Digital Single Market Directive 2019/790 and expressly reserve this publication from the text and data mining exception.

British Library Cataloguing-in-Publication Data
A catalogue record for this publication is available from the British Library.

Download the teaching notes and word cards to accompany this book at:
http://littlewandle.org.uk/signupfluency/

Get the latest Collins Big Cat news at
collins.co.uk/collinsbigcat

Author: Bali Rai
Illustrator: Debasmita Dasgupta
Publisher: Laura White
Commissioning editor and
 product manager: Caroline Green
Series editor: Charlotte Raby
Development editor: Catherine Baker
Project manager: Emily Hooton
Copyeditor: Sally Byford
Proofreader: Catherine Dakin
Cover designer: Sarah Finan
Typesetter: 2Hoots Publishing Services Ltd
Production controller: Katharine Willard

Printed in the UK.

MIX
Paper | Supporting responsible forestry
FSC™ C007454

This book contains FSC™ certified paper and other controlled sources to ensure responsible forest management.

For more information visit: www.harpercollins.co.uk/green

Made with responsibly sourced paper and vegetable ink

Scan to see how we are reducing our environmental impact.

Acknowledgements
The publishers gratefully acknowledge the permission granted to reproduce the copyright material in this book. Every effort has been made to trace copyright holders and to obtain their permission for the use of copyright material. The publishers will gladly receive any information enabling them to rectify any error or omission at the first opportunity.

p38 and p39 Eric Isselee/Shutterstock, p70t and b imageBROKER.com/Alamy, p71t Dinodia Photos/Alamy, p71b Associated Press/Alamy, p86 Svetlana Foote/Shutterstock, p87 Gulf MG/Shutterstock.